MW00917079

THE FALL GAUNTLET:

BEAR

BOOK ONE

J. A. MERKEL

— J. A. Merkel

A Worlds Apart Media Book
PUBLISHING HISTORY
Worlds Apart paperback edition / July 2023

Copyright © 2023 J. A. Merkel
Cover design by Roderick Brydon
All rights reserved

No part of this book may be reproduced or
transmitted in any form or by any means,
electronic or mechanical, including
photocopying, recording, or by any information
storage and retrieval system, without permission
in writing from the publisher.

ISBN: 979-8-9888120-0-5
Printed in the United States of America

For Jude,

No matter which universes we find ourselves in, I know time and time again, we'll be brothers every time.

CONTENTS

BEAR   i

ONE   1

TWO   9

THREE   19

FOUR   26

FIVE   32

SIX   37

SEVEN   45

BEAR

It is said that the bear disappeared from Calypso before many of the first animals; that among all the Originals, it sought out wisdom from the gods and goddesses before all others.

Would it be impossible to imagine that a creature so carefully crafted by the Deus would eventually seek out its creators? Or was the bear searching for something else?

Totem scholars believe that the bear never left our planet, that it is sleeping within the hollow of a great tree, waiting for its human champion to wake it from its slumber and bring protection to the land.

When the bear appears to you in a dream, listen to its steady breathing. Feel the beat of its one true and vicious heart. Learn the location of its sacrifice.

That is when the bear will awaken. That is when the bear lives inside you.

From the Book of Totems, Bear

J. A. MERKEL

ONE

In my nightmares, Soren and I are running. We're always running, but it's never fast enough. No one in my family can ever run fast enough.

On the morning of my final match, D rushes down the tunnel leading to my holding cell with the decisive and energetic footsteps I've come to know so well. She isn't supposed to be here, especially at five in the morning hours before my match, but I've stopped trying to figure out the Crown or anything about how the gods and goddesses work.

I put my lynx mask down on my desk and meet her at the door as her echoing steps die to nothing. She's out of breath, more hurried and rattled than I've seen her. "Has something happened? Am I still supposed to fight today?"

Pre-dawn light filters through the one barred window and casts deep shadows on her pale face as our planet tilts and opens itself to our star for the day. Another day of judgment. Her emerald-green eyes are hot with some unspoken pain, but her words are like ice. She is the one to carry the news of my brother, Soren, to me.

"He's been training for the Gauntlet, Benji," D says, catching her breath. "He's the one you have to fight."

Now I'm the breathless one.

Sometimes, you train for the better part of your life so you can save your mother from her off-world prison, and other times, you have to fight to the death against your own flesh and blood to free her.

I always thought Mom being arrested for treason and taken away was the beginning of the end, but in time I learned we would all pay for our sins: Dad, for the medicines we'd stolen to heal his infected and rotting leg from his accident at the mines; Soren, for breaking the leg of the Crown; and me, for orchestrating the heist.

That's the Crown for you—just when you think they've taken everything, they take more. And now they're doing it again.

Dad used to say that the Fall Gauntlet tournament was the Crown's way of maintaining public order by having people fight for what they believe in, while also pleasing the Deus, our all-knowing gods and goddesses—wherever they're supposed to be—but I'm beginning to think it's about something else.

The creators have been waiting for today, for the strongest fighter and totem animal to claim victory and rule over Harvest. At least for the next four years, until the next tournament happens and the cycle starts all over again. They'll grant the victor one wish, but—

Soren's been training for the Gauntlet?

My tongue feels like it's fallen down into my throat, but then I get the words out. "That wonderful and insightful piece of information would have been good

. . . oh, I don't know—seven years ago?" That's when Soren and I were separated from one another. Dad went to prison and we never heard from him again. Soren was sent to the mines at just eight years old to take Dad's place. Since I was skilled at ciantechnology by then, based on the contraptions I had made, they sent me to the inner circle to apprentice under Master Gherus, where I would make weapons and tech for the Crown.

D winces, swallowing the words I know she was ready to say, as she presses fingers against her temples. I know this is hard for her too. We've grown close during these last few months. She's been my confidante, a source of strength when I return to my cell, bringer of food, and speaker of mostly soothing words. This isn't her fault. The last thing I want is for her to feel bad about something she did or didn't tell me.

My entire family is being torn apart by the Crown, I'm about to battle my little brother to the death, and here I am worried about one of the Crown guards' feelings. Granted, she's not just any guard, but still— classic Benji move. This is probably why the Crown can control me with the promise of freeing my mother. Feelings.

"I'm sorry, Benji. I didn't know until now," D says. "One of the other guards was mouthing off, and they were going on and on about the bear champion, and they let the name Soren slip. I know you talked about him to me before. He's your final opponent." The words tumble out of her mouth like she doesn't have enough time. She steals a glance behind her. Maybe she doesn't.

"That doesn't get easier the second time you say it,"

I say.

"Benji, pull out. You can't fight against your brother—you can't beat the bear!"

D already knows that deserters are executed, so I don't remind her and instead indulge her small moment of hysteria. The Crown would never allow Soren or me to leave the Gauntlet because our nation needs a champion. A victorious bear means something very different for the people of the land than a victorious lynx.

I pick up my heavy lynx mask from my cot. I feel better holding it, being close to it—it helps me see what others cannot and has always been my key to victory.

Ignoring the fact that D thinks Soren can beat me in a fight, I say, "I need to see him. It's hard to believe you. That it's him. That he's here, fighting in this tournament too." I'm back at the cell door, looking into D's eyes, hoping there's some mistake.

Soren.

My only brother.

It's amazing what neural connections can do, because the second that I accept this news about Soren, my world opens to his presence, and memories of when we were last together rush towards me.

Light from the window skitters across the holding cell floor, but in another time, I'm seeing guards come through our door after one knock, as though these two realities are superimposed on one another.

Soren and I are escaping from a window. I'm waiting for Soren to land, to hurry up. Not hurried enough. A guard is intercepting us, grabbing me by the wrist, but then I'm turning his weight against him, bringing him down.

There's a rush of exhilaration, the unspeakable

satisfaction of besting someone I hate, someone who had already taken my mother away, and then the guard is on his feet, and my throat is in his hand, my back crushed against the stone wall, feet dangling, helpless. Soren is dropping down, finally. His eyes hold a golden glint, that first sign of rage that I knew even then would be our family's undoing.

Soren is punching once, twice, three times, and I'm telling him no, demanding that he stop. Soren is pausing, considering. I'm outmaneuvering the guard again, shooting my gripclaw into the wooden post above as I lasso his wrists and send him skyward, his bulky frame jerking off the ground like a fish on a hook.

The cool morning air is rushing past us as we sprint through the long and winding labyrinth that leads to home. Thoughts arrive, so many thoughts, a premonition, something warning me.

We should have been more careful.

We arrive home, throw open the door, excited to give Dad the medicine we've stolen, then—a silence so heavy it can crush your soul.

Two henchmen and a Gauntlet juror named Harmeny stand in our home. Harmeny is calling us thieves, telling us that thieves do not go unpunished under her watch. I'm thinking—knowing—that we should have never let the guard in the street see us.

There's a pang in my stomach for what Soren did, and I'm getting a sickening feeling, my stomach twisting into unrecognizable shapes, for what he is about to do.

He couldn't prevent it. Neither of us could prevent it. But Soren made sure to leave his mark.

My mind goes black.

"Benji, they say he kills people with one swing of his club," D says.

I don't respond.

I've heard stories and whispers over the years that Soren became angry and stupid, a ball of trapped energy refusing to learn how to read or return to the society he'd known.

It's hard to picture my brother and what he'd look like now, if he'd grown into a similar version of me, or if he'd reached the size and height Mom and Dad thought he would, tall and broad like a sailor. Like Poppy.

If he is the bear, he might be huge. I've never seen the bear, but I've heard about him. Part of me knew this is how it would end up, but the fact that my opponent is Soren is a shock I still can't process.

I wrack my brain for the lore behind the bear champion, trying to decipher what this matchup—lynx versus bear—will mean.

D is crying, and her hands are shaking as she presses them against her chest. Her tears are silent but carry years of pain over the Crown destroying lives like we are all just pawns on a chess board—expendable and insignificant.

The urge to shout at someone, something, anything, takes over. I want to tell D she's lying, that this is all a big trick, because what more could the Crown do to torture their citizens? What more could they do to torture me that they haven't already done?

They could feed me lies about my family, about the possibility of saving them, then pit me against my brother with only minutes to process the ordeal. It's been ten years since they took my mother, seven since they took my father and brother. Ten years of wondering and dreaming and wishing for a way to be with my family again, and this is how it happens.

"Are you in danger?" I ask her, aware of movement from new pieces in this grand chess game the Crown has constructed.

"Not that I know of." D shakes her head, brushing off my question. She looks up at me with bloodshot eyes. "How can the Crown be so cruel?"

I don't answer. I have to remain neutral, especially this close to my final match. A win means my wish will be granted and I can finally save Mom.

I'm so close to this victory, but now the Crown has chucked a rather large wrench into the works, clogging up and complicating what I've spent so many years building. I know I have to make a decision.

"What are you going to do, Benji?" D's eyes are bright with half-shed tears.

I hold up my mask as though it holds the answers that I need. With microchips and photosensors embedded into the interior, handiwork that I once learned while apprenticing for Master Gherus within the castle walls, the mask feels familiar, like it is the only ally I have in this fight.

Gherus taught me that I could become someone else with technology's help. By learning the principles of physics, by training to strengthen my muscles and perform maneuvers that would surprise and take down my opponents, I learned that I, too, could become a champion and make a wish to save the ones I loved. And if I didn't win, I'd die trying.

Placing the mask on my face will activate the aura field and release fission elements so that the mask's photon-receptors can create a more realistic image of a lynx. Once the organix have finished pixelating the holoskin, and my own internal system has calibrated to the mask's, integration will be complete. Removing my mask will result in immediate execution, since the identities of the fighters must always remain secret, so I'll need to figure out a way to show Soren—in case he doesn't already know—that he's fighting against his dear older brother.

Sure, easy enough.

The only other rule of the Gauntlet is that there can be only one champion. There are no draws.

"I'll do what I've always done," I say. "Defeat whatever the Crown throws at me."

I don't share with D what I'm really thinking.

I have no idea what to do.

TWO

Even from down here in the tunnels, I can hear the raucous stadium above me erupt with pre-match excitement; the thumping of sticks on goat-skinned drums, the boisterous, drunken laughter, and the wild, shrieking applause from the thousands of spectators create a collective and thunderous orchestra.

Several victories advanced me from the grunt rounds into the champion rounds. I'd chosen Gherus as my sponsor, so he was allowed to visit me at the time. Face to face, his eyes were soft and on the verge of tears. In the beginning, I was just an orphan on house arrest, the son of traitors using his skills to pay his debts to the Crown, but that was not what I was to Gherus by the end of my apprenticeship. A kind of orphan himself, we'd found that family was not only dictated by bloodline.

There was indecision in Gherus's eyes that day, but he was never too conflicted to give me advice that would save my life. "You have to consider what will happen in your final match, should you make it that far," he'd said. "There are many possibilities to consider."

"There's only one possibility," I'd said. "I'm going to save my mom."

Gherus dropped his gaze and his tone, his rapid speech revealing his anxiousness. "This isn't about what you want, Benji. This is, and has always been, about the Crown. This is about the world they've built and what they want. You are a pawn."

"A pawn that has almost reached the other side of the board," I'd said, slamming my fists against the cell door.

"We all have people we love," Gherus had said. "Do you think you're the only person looking to save someone?"

Now, on the other side of these walls, Soren is waiting for his platform to take him to the Gauntlet, just as I am waiting for mine. It's strange to think how much our lives have run parallel to each other, and yet I know nothing about him. Perhaps his time in the mines has made him a fierce, indestructible fighter. All these thoughts come to me in the dim light of the tunnels, as I stave off the scent of cool, musty air. I have traversed these tunnels dozens of times and as usual, I am alone.

I step onto my platform, but it does nothing. The hyrotech on the wall glows a neon orange to form an image of a mask. I hold my inactive lynx mask in my left hand, as though putting it on is acceptance of this fight.

News of Soren has my mind doing all sorts of things because now I'm thinking of the day I first entered the temple to speak my sacrifice to the Deus, in the hopes that I would be chosen for the tournament. They say the Deus choose their champions through the masks, Calypson vessels holding a portion of the gods' and goddesses' true power.

I'd lifted the dense, cold mask in my hands and stared into the lifeless eyes of the lynx, knowing that the totem animal was the closest match to my own spirit—a being of evolution and scientific discovery. If only I had known then that Soren would enter the temple at the hour of the bear, I could have prepared better for today.

My nerves were steel that day because I had nothing left to lose. Entering the tournament was the closest I'd ever get to the Deus, and winning was the only way I'd ever save Mom. I was either becoming the lynx now or never.

I placed the mask on my face while reciting the lynx's words and waited. Within the dark cave of the ancient device, the world became quiet, and then the Deus heard the sacrifice of my heart: my own life in exchange for the age-old tournament, and they—no, the lynx—chose me. The strength I felt then was otherworldly. The lynx's powers of precognition awakened and the temple exploded into a cosmic universe of probabilities that, at the time, I had no clue how to interpret.

Three months later, I understand my mask's abilities very well. As long as I live, the mask is codified to me and only I can wear it. Together, on this day of final judgment, only the lynx and I can activate this platform to take us to the arena. There are no stand-ins.

The creators have written it in the stars . . . or something like that.

Now or never, Benji.

The Crown will kill me if I don't engage, so I put it on like the good little fighter they want me to be. My body tightens like a hamstring in that first moment of mask transition like it always does, as my neurotransmitters stabilize and the o-tech calibrates to my own internal system; thousands of microsensors make contact with my skin, syncing with my brainwaves and locking into place with the larger structures of my meaty brain like parts of a two-pieced puzzle. I'm clenching my fists and gnashing my teeth as the human-mask integration roils on, the process combining genetics, psychohistory, and physiology, and the mask's superhuman abilities of prediction are plugged directly into my consciousness. The mask's boosted effect on my physiology, resulting in increased strength, agility, and reaction time, envelops my body like a laser scan and then it's over, burning off me in a wave of invisible heat. I feel thirty pounds stronger, but lithe like a lynx.

I grab my gem staff off the wall in front of me, the weapon paired with the lynx since the beginning of the Gauntlet, centuries before I was born. Anyone could pick it up and use it, but only organix activation—when the totem mask and its human match unite—unlocks its true potential. Nanoparticles coalesce to fortify the staff as it reaches its full height at six feet to match my own, the gemstone held in the crook at the end pulsing a cyan blue. The spark core is a thundercloud of potential energy, branching and spreading like the effervescent veins of leaves under glowlight. It doesn't seem like much when you're fighting against armored enemies with broadswords or serrated claws for hands, but the kinetic force that is created with movement can deliver a finishing blow with the right amount of power and technique.

The neon light in front of me morphs from orange to green and the system says in its feminine lilt, "Lynx identified. May you see the truth, always and forever." My platform rises.

The stadium floor opens above me as harsh sunlight presses against my suit. Now that my mask is on, the crowd will see the image and likeness of my lynx persona as the mask's micro hairs grow denser and my ears elongate until they form pointed tips. My skintight pants, lightweight boots which are more like the sandals of Hermes, strapped around my heels and calves, and a breathable mesh tunic fitted firmly to my body all help to increase my own aerodynamics.

The cacophony of sound is both dulled from within the cave of the mask on my face and augmented, voices and battle chants echoing through the cavernous expanse of sky above me. The humid air envelops me in its warm embrace as sweat runs down the back of my neck, and tiny hairs prickle against my lightweight garments. I can't stop the adrenaline now rushing through me as thousands of people wait for their new champion and an understanding of what this next Harvest will mean.

The last time the Gauntlet took place, I was only thirteen. The eagle had claimed victory, so Harvest followed the lore of our mighty winged predecessor.

The eagle summoned eastern winds meant to carry new life, pollination from other nations to grow new crops and trees and flowers. The winds would also power windmills that the Crown would build on farms. All that had happened when the eagle defeated the badger, a champion of grit, and a symbol of what it means to fight against something bigger than oneself.

It was easy to see which one of the two the Crown favored. I'll always remember how the badger fought that day, how it tried to break through the defensive winged shields of the eagle, only to be blown back again and again, until it could fight no more. The eagle delivered a finishing blow with its razor-thin wing blades, and the bloody, battered badger lost its head in a bloodcurdling moment that I'll never be able to unsee. At thirteen, I should have been more disturbed by it, but it felt like the natural progression of things. Violence seemed and still seems like the only way to get what you want in our cruel world.

And now they're turning flesh and blood against each other.

This death match of lynx versus bear is twisting my stomach into knots, and my platform has almost reached the stadium. Under the cloudless lapis-blue sky, spectators are clinking their drinks and drowning their sorrows in the veiled hope that their lives will be different tomorrow once there is a new champion.

A bear victory would spell four years of security and steady harvest in preparation for the long winter. The bear symbolizes a close connection to the ground, dirt, and soil, the land that feeds. The bear signifies overall protection and is, ironically, maternal in essence. Last I'd seen Soren, he was about as unmotherly as one could get. It makes sense, though, why people believe in the bear. The mother of mammals also represents protection against outside forces, and we've always been a nation all too aware of the rebel clans to the west. A victory from the bear during any other Gauntlet would be preferred, but not when it means my own death.

I can't allow the bear to win.

The morning sun beats down on me like a thousand hot needles, but I keep my eyes closed for now, focusing on my breath, on the nuances of sound and smell that will be my allies in this fight.

I need to focus on myself—on the lynx.

This is the first time the totem has become one of the sixteen champions. I represent a new path for the people of New Phasia: science. But since people's lives are on the line, novelty is synonymous with death. To most people, science is a scary word because it's something they don't understand. I have a hunch that the Crown has orchestrated this shielding of knowledge, but I have neither the time nor know-how to expose it. And besides, that isn't my destiny. If I win, it is the Crown's duty to generate new tech and identify new talent across the nation.

The lynx is the totem of high intellect and a desire to understand all that is known and unknown, which clashes like metal on metal with the people of New Phasia, who believe in working in the fields with their hands in the dirt.

My photon mask buzzes with a near-imperceptible electromagnetic frequency, and I'm bound to it then. It hugs my face like a mother I never really got to hold. Gauntlet champions have always been masked so the technology has been around for ages, but most people cannot recreate it, much less understand even the most basic principles of how phospho-imaging works.

The eyes of the lynx see the greater mysteries of life. As is my ritual of reviewing the lore of my opponent's champion, followed by my own, I touch the side of my photon mask and activate the hypo-ocular receptors built into the motherboard. The world explodes in a kaleidoscope of teals, oranges, indigoes, yellows and reds. The sudden shift is jarring, but I'm used to it now and can stomach the additional transition much easier than the first time. Light filters through, and the colors settle into layers as I parse them out into the reality unfolding before me.

I'm almost at the platform, which is raised one hundred feet off the ground. I peer down and see the spikes jutting into the air like giant shark teeth as deadly as a Megalodon's, the Crown's final assurance that only one champion survives.

My platform stops.

One more step across the gap and my final match begins. There he is. My heart catches in my throat, like a serpent trying to swallow a creature too large for it. The air is dry with heat, oppressive. Through the mask's openings, I take small sips of air with my mouth, exhaling through my nostrils. The twisting of my stomach tightens, and I am a mangled knot of fear and anger and love. The bear stands before me, and I don't even need to see behind the mask to know. I know it like the blood that runs through my veins, down to the marrow of my bones. Call it an energy.

D was right. My final match is against a brother I haven't seen or known in seven years.

My final match is against Soren.

The last time I saw Soren fight we were in our house in the Syphon District, which bordered the inner district, and was home to peasants like me and my family. Soren was a thin, raggedy child who stole food to keep up. It's hard to believe that I'm related to the fifteen-year-old in a bear mask facing me down like I'm the one who's taken his family away. I wonder if he knows what I know.

When I look at him and begin to intuit what he will

do, my visual receptors activate, and I see what no one else can. The crowd is witnessing two masked humans representing both a bear and a lynx, human-shaped with the ability to walk upright, but phospho-imaged to imitate those beasts, our masks morphing and sprouting hair, and our gauntlets growing retractable claws and fur. For as long as I focus my cerebral energy on seeing beyond the blurred illusion of holoskin that masks his features, I'll be able to see the real Soren underneath. I only need a moment.

Soren is big. He's at least a head taller than me, and broader in the shoulders. His forearms and legs are hairy, as though he's become part bear himself. My mask's main ability is probability precognition, meaning I can intuit mini futures based on probable outcomes in order to inform my choices. Its function is based on a complicated framework of neural pathways that are synced to the o-tech embedded in the mask.

Before Soren even moves, vector lines appear in my line of sight, parsing out all potential moves he could make as I absorb the probabilities related to each one. My aura field is an evolving grid of actions and reactions blended into a reality that I must constantly interpret. All these details and numbers strike me like mini bolts of lightning, zipping through the tundra of my mind, and I see him then in our apartment—the day I lost both him and Dad.

The memory tightens my throat and I'm seeing glimpses of my final moments with them in quick decisive bursts of light: Soren's bloody fists, his hot rage, the snap of bone as he swings his lead pipe at the guard, Juror Harmeny, the glint of a needle as she drives it into Soren's neck in an arc, and me, yelling and pleading for my Dad, telling them he's too old and broken to work for the Crown. I was the one who stole. It was my idea, so take me instead!

I knew the survival rate of miners; I knew what imprisonment by the Crown meant.

Harmeny's warm voice instilled a hate in me that has never died. "But you are not the one with the rage. Don't worry, child—I have different plans for you."

All of it, the fierce light being sucked away from our home as they left me in darkness, the shouts from Soren, the blood—comes together in a whirling image.

Soren is a different person now. That day his rage was unbound and dangerous; today it will be turned against me.

Unless I do something about it.

The announcer's voice snaps me from my reverie. "Ladies and gentlemen, have we got a match for you. Welcome to the final round of the Fall Gauntlet—lynx versus bear!"

THREE

As the stadium erupts with cheers and shouts, all I can think about is how I've put everything into this moment.

I've trained with Master Gherus and learned everything I could about the 3-D nanoparticle projection capabilities of phosphotech, the algorithmic, raw computing power of ciantech and its embedded microchips, and my favorite, what I began to learn firsthand through mask integration—the fission elements and their ability to power o-tech and its endlessly complex mechanisms—so that I could one day be strong enough to fight in the Gauntlet and bring my mother back with a single wish.

I've fought like an animal that knows each fight may be its last, and it was a choice I made willingly. I've been clobbered to the point of blacking out, beaten and bruised until my body was a black and blue balloon. I've ended a life with a gem staff blow to the head. I'm not just clever anymore with my technology and ability to make connections. I can see and guess beyond the present moment and have become a fighter, the fighter I've always wanted to be. I've made it past the grunt rounds where so many skilled fighters fall and die to become one of sixteen champions, then on to the finals, only to find out that perhaps combat and survival is in our family's blood.

My body is relaxed and at ease, falling into a quiet calm that overtakes me and allows instinct to drive. My mind is on the brink of utter disarray, fractured, communicating with my heart in weak, tampered signals, and all of me is about to come undone.

I hear D's voice in my head. "You have to pull out."

I can't think straight. I shouldn't be thinking at all because thinking gets you killed. "You have to just act," Master Gherus had said. "You have to let instinct guide you."

Is that what I'm supposed to do? Tap into the ever-flowing fountain of wisdom that I was graced with? It doesn't matter. Wisdom is irrelevant now.

I need to act and be one step ahead.

Our match begins. As I step onto the arena my thoughts show me the main component of our "floating" platform, held up by long chains attached to the four corners of the massive block of sandstone. I've always known it, but today my mask is showing me the camo tech that gives the crowd the visual enjoyment of a floating isle.

Across from where I stand, one hundred feet away, Soren steps onto the battle arena. My mask's aura field activates, and I ingest all the probabilities related to his potential actions. Each one carries more weight than I've ever known as the blue lines disperse, retract, then branch into new pathways all leading to one single outcome: Soren's death, or my own.

I don't know if the bear knows who he's fighting or not.

The vectors display a quick burst of micro movements that I've come to understand as certain emotions, so my guess is he doesn't. Based on his strong, decisive steps forward, my intuition tells me he'll have no qualms about killing me. I now know that Soren did not receive the same kind of information that I did.

That's where it gets complicated.

I need him to know who I am so that he doesn't kill me, but I'm also not allowed to remove my mask—one of the two Gauntlet rules—so I'll need to tell him in words. Then comes our next dilemma: if neither of us wins, then it's a draw, which isn't technically against the rules, but there has to be a winner. The Crown will accept nothing less, and it's clear to me now that they've orchestrated this outcome. It's too perfect. Brother versus brother. They want to see this match play out just as much as our people do, but for different reasons—reasons I haven't yet figured out.

It doesn't matter though, because Soren is approaching me. His giant gauntlets with their metal claws gleam in the piercing autumn sun with every step as he grips a massive, spiked club that he could use to slaughter a whale.

I step forward to meet him but now the vectors are inverting and collapsing within the aura field, and I digest the minute probability that I will have to raise arms against Soren and strike him dead. The vision shows me striking him with the gem of my staff over and over, quick and merciless. I'm getting sick thinking about it. I can't do it, so I pull away from the vision. The Crown wants me to, but I can't. I'd save Mom upon victory, but something about this isn't right. Gracious goddess—nothing about this is right.

I don't have time to decide what is right, only to dodge Soren's first attack. He swings his massive club at me, once, twice, as I duck under the first and jump over the second. I start to swing my staff but can't gain momentum because he lunges at me again, his claw cutting through the air with enough velocity to slice me open. I intuit to see the odds of his movements, glimpsing and attaching to a deceleration of his latest jab, giving me enough time to sidestep away from him and into the captured insight. My guess is correct. He's open to attack, so I kick his inner thigh, once, twice, then rap my gem staff against the crook of his elbow. He groans, tries to shake it off, but he can't. I've hit a pressure point.

The bear's eyes are hell inside his mask, the skin around them pulsing violet. He isn't stunned anymore, so he swipes at me with his other hand.

"The bear does not hesitate, and yet he is!" the announcer says. The crowd takes in a collective breath, experiencing a minor bout of confusion as they realize that their chosen hero is not perfect.

Now that I'm close enough to see Soren's eyes, I feel more of him, my brother, his innocence ripped from him, all the rage he's held onto and has never released. Defeating me won't help. It never helps. I push down the beginnings of bile in my throat, my skin crawling at the thought of one of us dying today.

I need Soren to know it's me.

Stepping back and away with lithe movements and no clue of what I will do once Soren sees me—I'll probably be executed for breaking the rule, but it's better than having to murder my brother—I grab my mask under the chin and pull.

It won't budge. It's held in place as if by sap.

Soren is back, swinging. Above the crowd, his voice is clear, booming, no longer the voice of a young boy. "Your death is the fate of our people. Accept it."

It's one of the bear's incantations. The words strike me with more force than a club to the chest. I falter. He seizes the opening, grabbing me by the neck like I'm a slab of meat that he can squeeze the blood from.

I'm in Soren's death grip, and yet the Crown holds both of us in theirs. Breaking his stronghold on me is the first step in breaking their hold on my family and our nation.

"Soren!" I manage to say with a collapsing trachea.

His nostrils flare. He loosens his grip enough for me to steal a breath.

I throw my weight forward and kick up, my boot slamming against his skull. He releases me enough for me to land and back away toward the edge to catch my breath.

"How did you—" he says.

Before, all I saw was a bear hellbent on spilling blood, and now I see a hurt, injured human, fighting for something as well. I haven't had time to think about what Soren might wish for. Now, he's calculating who I am, how I know his name, how this lynx is able to say something in a voice so similar to the brother he once had.

Soren is not prepared for this truth hurtling towards him.

He cannot fathom that I could be here now.

The Crown has done something to my mask to make sure I can't remove it. They're one step ahead. They know that if either of us shows our faces, we'll drop our arms and refuse to fight. They broke Soren and turned him into their lapdog, but they cannot come between brothers. Not brothers like Soren and me.

I know more about the masks than the common champion since I had helped build some of the phospho-imaging tech in them. You can deactivate the masks, canceling out the image that they project onto the person, by tripping the sensors, which can be done by overheating them. Once deactivated, I'll also be able to remove it.

"The Crown said my opponent would try to trick me, the lynx especially."

The Crown has already gotten to him, and I'm wondering how deep the trust goes, but I have more pressing matters to worry about.

Soren bounds forward in a rage. I stand my ground. He swings his claw at me, which I dodge, but then he does exactly what I want him to do next—he sweeps his claw in a backhand motion. Turning ninety degrees so that my torso takes the brunt of the attack, I use the force of his swipe to launch myself onto the ground, making sure to keep the temple of my mask pressed to the platform. My entire body sings out in pain as I slide across the arena.

I lose track of time, of the sounds around me, and stagger to my feet. I'd underestimated Soren's power and now my torso is cut open and gushing blood. I grimace, holding the wound. It was my only option. I fall to one knee and feel around for the tiniest latch on the inside of the mask, which will release it from my face as long as the sensor has been tripped.

Soren is bounding forward again. The announcer is blathering on that my final moments have come. Not today.

I tear my mask from my face, and this time it comes off clean. The warm air sucks the breath out of my lungs. I've lost my powers of precognition, my staff is now heavier than I can hold, and it feels like I'm suddenly naked in a room full of strangers, devoid of even an ounce of power.

The entire stadium falls silent.

I've just broken a Fall Gauntlet rule, and everyone sees that I—Benji Calyx—am the lynx. I don't care. As long as Soren knows, I've accomplished my mission. If he still wants to kill me now, then there's nothing I can do to get him back.

The bear runs forward, ready to swing his club to knock my head clean off, but stops dead in his tracks. He's clocked who I am, like I am a ghost returned from the past.

His shoulders drop and his hands fall to his sides. He draws in a long breath, like his body cannot process this moment. The rage is still there, but there is something else too. He leans forward and I can smell his hot breath, sticky with the scent of rice and stale coffee.

"Benji?" he asks.

FOUR

everal moments pass before anyone reacts, and
then—utter chaos.

The stadium erupts into a cacophony of
sound, as anger rips through the warmed air like a
hurricane. People shout and throw garbage at the arena
with betrayal in their hateful and confused cries, a
betrayal of what people of the land have come to see
on this final day of the tournament.

"The lynx has unmasked himself!" the announcer
says. "Our masked marauder has revealed his true
identity."

It doesn't matter. I don't care who knows me.
Winning has become irrelevant. It would have saved
my mother, but the Crown has turned it into
something I could never live with.

"What . . . is this?" Soren asks. His eyes are like
amber diamonds behind his well-crafted mask, and I
sense the universe of sadness swirling inside them.
"How did you—?" Soren turns with a sharp movement
to look at the crowd, as though this is their fault. Maybe

it is.

"Is the lynx playing some kind of mental game?" the announcer asks.

People in the stadium are booing us now, throwing wads of garbage. Objects pepper the intense sunlight like a random swarm of insects flying at us.

"Soren," I say while watching him, trying to anticipate what will come next, even without my mask. I think that I know him. I want to know him again, but the truth is, I don't know what he will do.

I run from the landslide of thoughts in my brain, trying not to be crushed by the weight of it. They can't force us to murder each other.

"We have to get out of here," I say. "Escape together. The Crown has been planning for us to meet like this for years." I don't know the truth of that statement, but the clues are coming together now, and they seem irrefutable. It's at least a seed for Soren to chew on, and that's a start. I don't know how to communicate with this brother that has been taken from me.

Everything happens fast after that. Our voices are drowned out by the people, some of them once loyal to the lynx, and some of them still loyal to the bear, who has not revealed his identity.

"What will the bear do now that the lynx is just a man?" the announcer asks.

Soren's grip tenses around his club. Inside his gauntlets, his hands tighten into fists. Maybe he's so far gone, brainwashed by the very people who've destroyed his life that he no longer knows me, and has no problem striking me down. But then he says, "How can we escape? The Crown is everywhere."

I've reached some part of him. He's questioning.

He's always been curious, open-minded in ways that used to surprise me, interested in justice, curious about all angles. It is fitting that he is the bear, the totem with the ability to pass between the spirit realm and ours.

"Stand down," I say. "If you stand with me in solidarity they have to fight us both."

"They'll kill us," Soren says, but his voice exudes no fear. "I don't understand how you're here. They told me you were—" Soren's head drops a hair's breadth. He loosens his hold on his club, then as if to let everyone know where he stands in this fight, he releases hold of his gauntlets. They fall to the ground with a thud. His bare hands are even more menacing than the gauntlets twice their size.

The fight is over. For now. The announcer stalls and drones on about there never having been a match like this.

Don't I know it.

Metalmen are there the next instant, cuffing us and leading us back to our platforms, back down to the tunnels to return to our holding cells. I don't know what will come next, but I can guess.

"The Crown locked my mask," I tell D as soon as she visits me once I am back in my cell. She doesn't come with food like she usually does after a match, but then again, I haven't won.

"Benji, how did you break the code?" D asks. Her question is focused and informed, and there is something in her eyes that says she knew this would happen. How does she know that the masks have codes? It's not common knowledge, and I've never talked about my ciantech days, but then again, there is a lot about D that I don't know. In fact, now that I watch her moving the blonde hair out of her eyes, her emerald-green eyes piercing my soul like the talons of a dragon, I realize that I don't know much about D at all.

The lynx's greatest strength is being able to see all that is known and unknown.

Under the tutelage of Master Gherus, I learned to never trust or believe anyone, and now I'm wondering who or what to believe, if Soren was merely playing a part, or if the Crown is, again, two steps ahead. I decide not since they didn't anticipate me breaking the code to their mask mid-battle.

"I just did," I tell D. "I had to reveal myself to Soren."

"It may have bought you some time, but . . ."

I watch D, trying to intuit how she's come across select information. Part of me is tempted to put my mask back on so I can see even more, but too much of the neurosync can fry my neurons, so I decide against it.

D says, "If neither you nor Soren win in the next match, they're going to kill you both. Public execution."

"How do you know?"

"I heard the other guards talking."

I track her eye movements, trying to detect any sign of a lie. I find nothing. "So what am I supposed to do?" I see Master Gherus in my mind's eye, in our days of apprenticeship, me at my station, tinkering, him shuffling over to inspect my handiwork, asking why I attached a wire in such an unconventional way, or why I couldn't do things the way others had done it before me. I try to think of what he'd tell me to do. "Escape?" I ask D, as if she is a substitute for my wise teacher.

"Benji?" D says, and I can sense she has more to

say.

I meet her eyes and see death in them, like she has seen it before and knows its shape and color. A darkness creeps across the horizon of her bright eyes. "What else did you hear, D?"

"It's about your dad."

A deep sigh leaves my body. I don't want the Crown pulling anyone else in my family into this ordeal, but I'm afraid my wishes mean nothing at this point.

"He had a wish too."

"Oh?"

"His wish was to save his own life. In exchange, he was tasked with moving the pieces that would set you and Soren against each other today."

My mouth falls open. I don't know what the truth is anymore—what is real and what the Crown has invented to destroy my family further. My throat tightens. I don't want to believe it. Who wants to believe that their father would betray them, give them away to the Crown dogs in exchange for his own life?

But then I remember my father and the last time I saw him when my mother was still with us. How he cowered and said nothing as they took her away. I try to separate what I want to believe and what is truth, but it's getting harder these days.

Now I realize what our family meant to the Crown, what we represented. I never learned enough about what Mom was planning to know the level of threat she presented. But I knew that Soren and I had not advanced to the final round of the Gauntlet by chance. Even now, we would pay for the sins of our traitorous parents.

I have a plan, but I'm going to need some time.

"When do we go again?" I ask D.

She shakes her head as though the next match will be even worse than the first. "I don't know, but I'll find out."

D leaves my cell, and I wrack my brain for solutions to my problem, playing out every possible scenario now that Soren is an integral piece in this puzzle. What would Gherus tell me now? How would he approach this life-or-death anomaly? I turn back to my makeshift desk, a slab of stone built into the wall with a wooden stool underneath, the giant book of lore lying closed like a tome of secrets on top. Gherus would tell me that the Crown is not a complicated entity. They have power and control, but the clues as to how they will make their next move are all there.

Approaching my desk and staring at the rows of totems on the front of the book, I know there must be some answer for me inside. I open the heavy book to the lynx totem and start reading as I've done thousands of times. This time, I am looking for something different.

FIVE

My candle is flickering to its final flames by the time I look up from the totem lore.

My eyes burn. The lynx lore I know by heart, but I had to reread parts about the bear. I haven't familiarized myself with the other totems because I thought it would distract me from my mission. Anything that doesn't help me win is a distraction. But this will help me win. Knowing that my final opponent is the bear and having a second chance to think about what the match means is a gift. One the Crown does not readily give. I know what they'll do next. One of us has to win, and if neither of us delivers the finishing blow, they'll force one of us to. After all this time, they have to have a champion. The nation depends on it. The question is, which one of us do they favor?

When D returns, I'm weary from reading, but the darkness I now find myself in is somehow soothing. D carries an oil light, and I see defeat in her eyes, as if she's been admonished since I'd last seen her hours before. "Your match is a week away," she says.

This is the norm between matches so that the champions can rest, but Soren and I haven't really fought or injured each other at all, so a week seems unnecessary. "A week? I can't wait a week."

"Benji, you can't believe anything I say," D says. Shadows dance across her face, and I can't fully read her expression.

"Should I believe that?" I know the Crown's tricks, and this might be of them.

"I'm serious," D says.

"Then why say anything at all?"

D hesitates. She's been roped into this tournament as my confidante and may have been chosen based on our compatibility. Our relationship has never been romantic for me, because I don't have time to think about that, but she grows softer each time she comes to visit me. She's no longer just the guard of my holding cell. She's invested in my success. "I keep overhearing things, and I think it's a setup. They want me to hear and tell you."

"To confuse me and throw me off course?"

"Maybe."

I grab at the fine hairs on my chin. "Keep telling me. I'll decide what's true or not. I am the lynx, after all. What did you hear this time?"

D sighs. "Your stunt of revealing your identity angered the Crown."

"No surprise there."

"The people know that you and Soren must have known each other. Now people are wondering if the Gauntlet has always been about pitting loved ones against each other."

Are Soren and I the exception or the rule?

"You have to think about other champions that

have won."

"Everyone knows the eagle won last time," I say.

"What happens to them after?" D asks.

"No one knows," I say.

D looks at me, her eyebrows raised. She waits.

"They don't live, do they?"

"Their wish may come true," D says. "They may live, but their lives are not theirs."

"So the Crown owns them."

"That's all I know," D says, releasing a sigh, as though holding those truths inside her was too much, and now she can breathe again.

I'm taking it all in as Mom, Soren, and Dad swim through my thoughts. What will happen to each of us? Will any of us ever be together again? Closing my eyes, I try to breathe and focus on the next match as I always have. I don't see how it's possible to get out of this alive. I can't have everything that I want. Saving Mom means killing Soren, but what does saving Soren and myself look like?

"Can you get a message to Soren, D?"

She shakes her head. "I don't know where he's being held. I think he's under the Crown's control, Benji."

I need help, but Soren is right—the Crown is everywhere, all knowing, ruling with their iron fist and steel blade. What can I do? The only powerful entities are the Crown or the totems.

"D, what shifts the tides of battle?" I need to talk out loud, move through this problem with someone else.

"It's hopeless, Benji. The Crown has thought of everything. If you shift the tides of battle, you win. If Soren does, he wins. His wish is to save your father."

"How do you know that?"

"I heard it, like everything else."

"So he may kill me."

"I don't think he has a choice."

"We always have a choice." The Crown wants me to strike him down. This information that D brings to me, true or not, is carrying me closer to my own truth. Out of the two of us, the Crown not only favors the totem whose lore will rescue the people, they favor the brother who is easier to manipulate.

The facts begin slamming into me like meteorites. Soren may be the Crown's lapdog, but they can't extinguish his rage. I saw it in his eyes. If he wants to, if he goes berserk again, he can murder whomever he wants. Under the tutelage of Gherus, I had been the Crown's dog too. I'd made them weapons and masks and new tech. I was the easier of the two brothers to control. I was the totem favored to win. My victory means four years of the sciences, something the Crown has always been hesitant to introduce to their people, but perhaps they need it now. Perhaps I am the answer.

But winning is playing right into their hand. I also have to get Soren out, and I'm beginning to get an idea.

"There is no power without the Crown," D says at last. "They're a black hole sucking in all light."

"The eagle effected change because the people believed and followed. What would the Crown be without its people following?"

D stares at me, and her eyes well up with a newfound misery. "And how do you expect to get the people to follow you and not the Crown?"

I think for a moment, recalling what I've just read about the lynx and the bear. There are so many tiny details that could carry weight if executed correctly.

"Okay. Soren is out, but there's someone else I need you to get a message to."

"I have a feeling the Crown will be watching what I do," D says.

"Then you'll have to be careful. Sounds like we have plenty of time."

SIX

There are some things more painful than death.

Not that I've died before.

The week before my second matchup against Soren was torture. Every morning, D would come to me with more news, and I was beginning to think that I shouldn't believe anything she said. That everything she heard was part of some larger plan to unhinge me. The Crown is no stranger to psychological torment, and based on what I was hearing, I was worried about what they were feeding to Soren.

I've become mentally tough because I had Gherus's support and I've adopted healthy coping strategies, but I don't know if Soren ever has. His coping strategies come from anger, from kicking guards and breaking their bones, which is what got him taken away in the first place.

By the time I enter the stadium, I've detached myself from all information. All that matters is what I'm going to do. I can't make any mistakes today. A single one could cost me my life, or Soren's.

I couldn't reach him during our week of solitude, so I had to rely on our brotherhood, our shared love for each other and our family, for my plan to work. Cold, brilliant sunlight tickles my exposed skin when my platform reaches the arena. Soren stands across from me, and I see the depth of his bear persona. His mask is menacing with its round, knowing eyes, bared teeth, pointed ears, and coarse hair covering the cheeks. The veins in his arms bulge, almost reptilian. His muscles are twice as big as mine.

"Ladies and gentlemen, we return for the final match of our Fall Gauntlet," the announcer says, his voice profound and perfect with the help of the voice amplifier. The air is crisp, colder than it was a week ago as our planet enters the autumn season. "The lynx will face off against the bear, and there shall be only one victor."

Soren and I step onto the arena in sync, and I try to intuit what he might be thinking. If his wish is truly to save Dad, I wonder who—if this is an accurate litmus test—he loves more. Perhaps he's had contact with Dad over the years or has been made to believe that he is close to saving him. There is something in the way he stands, with his chin tucked to his chest, revealing no neck, no sign of weakness, that makes me question everything about this past week and my own plan.

Would he really kill me to save Dad?

The time for thinking is over. I fumble with the voice piece in my pocket, the final gift given to me by D mere hours before the match. If science and knowledge are the way of the lynx, then I shall use my voice to challenge the Crown's. All I need is for Soren to sit still long enough to not attack me while I deliver my message.

It doesn't happen quite like that.

As soon as I pull out the voice piece, Soren is on me. He barrels forward as though on his paws, then swipes at me, claws out and sharpened. I back away, clutching my voice piece, tucking it back into my pants where it will be safe.

"Soren! You have to work with me!"

He stands tall, then lunges at me with all his weight forward. I'm near the edge, and could, with the appropriate footwork, invade his center of gravity and put him in a compromised position: off-balance, momentum racing forward to the point that I could send him careening off the edge. But I can't.

Instead, I sidestep, then dance around his jabs, just out of range, scanning his eyes, where his mind might be. He doesn't respond to me, doesn't even acknowledge that I've said anything, and now he's given himself away.

"The bear will do anything to protect its people," the announcer says. "He knows the winter will be hard, and he will be the protector."

Soren is in a mild state of his signature berserk mode, and I know that his mission—whether he's chosen this himself or not—is to end me, which in turn will push me to end him, thus playing right into the Crown's plan. Now I'm sure of it. I've seen the look in his eyes, the same look he had when they took Dad away. The Crown has commandeered his behavior, and I need to do exactly as Harmeny did that day and knock him out. But only for a minute. I need him to walk out of here on his own two feet with me.

He's at the edge now, and I have the advantage.

I swing my staff at his neck, which he's still protecting. He swipes those wild and massive claws at me, and I feel the rush of wind against my chest and my torso as he moves again and again against me. It becomes a flurry of swings and swipes, the staff of science and knowledge versus paws of grit and might. When they clash, there are sparks of light, glinting off the metal blades in his claws as they collide with the rhodamium in my staff's gemstone. The people are shouting and cheering.

I've lost some muscle definition during the week, spending more time on reading than on push-ups and planks, and Soren seems to have doubled in strength, like he's been eating all week. He's full, near bloated, his muscles holding maximum water, and I've leaned out even more. It's not always about strength, though. Sometimes it's about precision. Getting the right message to the right people at the right time.

Or striking when there is an opening.

Soren leaves one as he swipes in a backhand motion, his temple exposed. I step on his arm to launch myself high into the air, pull my staff back behind my shoulder, then drive it at his temple. The mask cracks. I land and back away, making sure to put plenty of distance between us. He's in berserk mode because of the mask, and now I've cracked whatever code had him in his straitjacket of servitude.

He staggers backward, tries to readjust his mask, but I'm already speaking into the voice piece.

"People of New Phasia!" My voice is hoarse. I'm not used to addressing this many people at once, but the amplifier carries it well enough.

The shouts of the crowd go from sheer anger and rage to mild confusion, as though their hopes and fears have been dampened by sudden rain. I know the announcer wants to speak, but he has never seen anything like this, and he's trying to see how it will go. What he'll need to do to control the situation. He's not nobody. With the power of voice in my hands now, I know that he stands for the Crown's power today and throughout the tournament. Whoever can get the message across holds the power.

"The lynx thinks he can whisper words to you so that he doesn't have to fight," the announcer says.

I'm prepared for this tactic and bend it to my own plan. "And the Crown wants my brother, Soren—the bear—and I to fight, so that they never have to. When you think of the Crown, who do you see?"

The crowd has fallen silent. Only the soft wisp of wind blowing through the arena can be heard. The sounds of trumpets and drums have died out. It is so quiet that my voice echoes for a moment through the stadium. The vector field in my line of sight is exploding into a wild amalgamation of probabilities and ratios that are too overwhelming to parse out. I press on.

"You don't see anyone because the Crown is the ultimate coward. Their faces are our"— and I point to my mask and then to Soren—"our faces. And for as long as you live, this is how it will always be. Fighter versus fighter. Loved one versus loved one. Fighting to the death so that they can exact upon their people whatever new prophecy will fit their agenda, year after year. Well, I ask you, my people—my lynx and my bears, not one or the other—I ask all of you, brothers and sisters, who will truly have your back in the end: your own flesh and blood, or the Crown?"

"The lynx has gone a little crazy," the announcer says. "He's spent too much time in his tunnels, don't you think?"

The crowd remains silent.

"So I ask you in these final moments where the Crown has asked you to play witness to brothers who have been pitted against each other over the past seven years, who have been separated from each other, each made to believe that the other is dead, one brainwashed to believe that saving his mother is the only way forward, and the other made to believe that saving his father is the only way forward. People of New Phasia, if you have a loved one out there serving the Crown, or secretly groomed to fight in the next Fall Gauntlet, then ask yourself: What else have you got to lose? I know there are those out there who would choose the people—not the lynx or the bear, but both—as a new reality and way forward. The old way of one champion and four years of Harvest will not yield anything new. The only way to change our lives moving forward is to break this pattern and stand up against the Crown. To stand up with me and my brother!"

I fall silent, trying to catch my breath, blacking out some of these last moments, as my mind tries to comprehend what I am doing, this tactical interruption that will be my death or my life.

Now's the time.

Soren is adjusting his mask, regaining his balance, his brainwashed thoughts and feelings fed to him by way of the mask now in question.

"If you are with me, then fight with me. End the voice of the Crown and their tyranny by overtaking the announcer's box. Father of the lynx and mother of the bear, show yourselves and do what you have always wanted to do."

My final message must have gotten to an old friend of mine, because the supposed standing leaders of the lynx and the bear make moves to storm the announcer's box.

Everything happens so fast.

I've gotten my messages across, and the wave that will become the first riot in the history of the Fall Gauntlet begins as a curtain moving and falling upon us. Dark clouds storm overhead, and droplets of rain fall on my head, cooling my skin. Will the Deus see what I'm doing and interfere? Soren lunges for me again, but I sidestep and hit the crack that I've already created in his mask, making it bigger. It connects and his mask falls to the ground with a thud.

"Soren, you have to come with me!"

I know he's been brainwashed because when he looks at me, his eyes wide and bewildered, shaking off the power that has been controlling him, he seems ready to break.

"Benji?" It's like he's seeing me again for the first time. The Crown has done something to his memory. "What . . . is this?" He wants to break down and cry, but I can't let him.

"We're going now, Soren. Follow me!"

He's lost a part of his mind, but the part that is still there sees that his brother has come back to save him.

I run to the arena's corner and as if on cue, the chains that hold up the platform appear, materializing out of thin air, the camo tech disabling, allowing us to see their true form. They connect to the platform's corners and then run up and over the stands to giant pillars behind the stadium. The chains are wide and sturdy—not the perfect escape route, but better than what is below. I step onto the chain and look behind me at Soren's dazed expression. His skin is pale, ghastly even, like this choice of escape is worse than death.

"Follow me, Soren. Hold onto me if you need to."

"What are we doing?" Soren yells at me, his voice gruff and gravelly from disuse.

"We're going to save Mom and Dad. And we're going to do it our way."

Soren says nothing, just stares at me wide-eyed, as though he's not sure if I'm someone he can trust yet, this brother that he hasn't seen in so long. But the promise of saving Dad may be enough for him to trust me for now.

His giant bear claw touches my gauntlet, and we hold each other in place. As a feline totem, balance has never been a problem for me. Soren couldn't do this alone, not now, I know, but he's with me.

"But the Crown," Soren says. "They'll find us. Kill us."

"Doesn't seem any different than any other day," I say, starting to scale the chains, leading Soren along. "Let them try. I'm not leaving you again."

SEVEN

The day the Crown took Mom away was a dark one for our family, but it wasn't until they took Dad and Soren that life really changed.

For years I secretly tried to find out what happened to Mom. Since she was named a traitor, it would have been dangerous to talk or ask about her openly. When Dad and Soren left, I knew what happened to them, but somehow they seemed more distant than Mom. Maybe they died in my mind that day because I knew the Crown controlled them. With Mom, I always believed she'd be fighting back in her own way.

The guard who took her away said that Mom was going to an off-world prison. I knew that there were other planets and galaxies in the great beyond, but I had no knowledge of what they were or where they might be. I had no knowledge of any ships or spacecraft that we had on Calypso, but then again, I had no knowledge of the tech the Crown was using until I was inside the castle walls making some of it myself.

The day Dad and Soren were taken, I spent the entire night thinking of what I could do to get Mom back. I spent that first night alone, in a paralyzed, blind rage, my thoughts rushing through the twisted labyrinth of my mind. Later, I learned that I was experiencing a new kind of trauma, compounding and more powerful than the first, which was causing my brain to stretch and grow in new ways. There were fires burning new neural networks and pathways, so of course, I did not sleep.

When Harmeny returned the next day, her eyes twinkling with an insatiable hunger for new lives she could undo, I went willingly to my trial, because what else could I do? I was a different boy, hardened by the long, cruel night and the repeated images of Soren and his wild eyes, the lead pipe slashing through the air, glinting like a beastly claw, and then the sickening snap of bone. Haunted by the images of Dad hobbling off, his own ruined leg forever on the verge of healing just enough to only be broken but destabilized by perpetual infection. The medicine we'd stolen was intended to save his life, for we knew very little about the lifecycles of bacteria and infection at our ripe ages of ten and eight.

I stood trial for my crimes, for orchestrating a heist from a clinic, breaking and entering, accomplice to assault and battery, and a long list of other irrefutable grievances. My sentence was not the mines like Soren, who'd need to temper his anger, and what better place than the claustrophobic, soul-crushing darkness of the underground? My sentence was not the servitude that my father would face, although I did not know what happened to him at the time. No, my sentence would be dedicated to science in service of the Crown.

Harmeny had seen my talents—she often congratulated herself for being a people person—with the gripclaw she'd learned had helped me climb during my days as a thief. She saw that I had potential in making things. Even things the Crown had not yet made.

When I'd learned about the Fall Gauntlet, about the wish granted to champions, about Harvest and the four-year cycles that each totem initiated upon victory, I began bending my studies to my own will. I learned as much as I could from Gherus during our time together and created weapons and devices for the Crown without error. I also began to learn things for myself.

And now, as Soren and I tread on the now-visible chains that will be our escape out of the stadium, I know I will need to learn many more things. Like how to run and escape from a ruling body that would have our heads for breaking the totem cycle and starting a revolution.

The crowd's screams reverberate in my ears as I try to lead Soren higher on the chain. His careful steps are not cat-like, nimble, and lithe like mine, but more rooted to things of the ground. Still, he's making it okay, just like he did when we'd scale buildings. It would take him longer than me, but he'd always get there.

The shouts encircling us are warlike. Battle cries balloon and collapse within the arena as though we are in a bubble. I do not know if people are dying or if this is more of a demonstration of strength, a symbol of what the bears and lynx can do if they team up and fight back.

Sweat pours down my forehead and arms. I still

wear my mask, but Soren does not. Those looking close enough could see the resemblance: the round, full face and angular jaw, the same dark hair, cut short, the same determined look in our light eyes—mine sea blue, his amber—thirsty to bring back those taken from us.

It is the look of a survivor, a pained warrior, a maker of change.

We're at the stadium's upper lip before I know it. The gauntlet arena looks clean and inviting from here, the demarcation lines on the battle platform black and neat. So many battles fought, so many useless deaths. Could I have done anything differently?

I step off the chain and onto the stadium wall wide enough for half my foot. I pull Soren to me in a great sweep as I sidestep to give him room. Grabbing his bicep, I hold his giant frame in place, steadying us both. He's still shaky, still unsure of these jarring changes in the course of his history.

"Soren!" I shout above the barrage of noise below me and all around. "We need to leave the city. The South Gate is closest, so we'll pass through there. We need to move. They'll be locking us in soon if they haven't already. Are you ready for this?"

The hesitation in Soren's eyes is a universe all its own. His pupils are dilating like crazy, taking in new light, and I sense the slightest shake in his body, like he used to do when he slept. He breathes deep through his nose, and his chest rises and falls like the cataclysmic shifting of tectonic plates. He knows his next move will send shockwaves through our lives. He does not use words, only nods his large head, and I know it's time to run like hell.

We find chains on the back wall and scale down,

like we did when we stole for Dad.

On the ground, the gates are already closed like I thought they might be, but they're accompanied by chaos. People are running through the labyrinth of streets, a crisscross of movement, some of them retreating, cowering in fear, others with stolen goods or handheld blades or shields.

When we stop to catch our breath after five minutes of running without stopping, I feel a sense of victory— though I know it is small and only the beginning of our struggles—wash over me. It fills me with such gusto that I don't know how to contain it or process it. This is the first time I've stood up to the Crown, and right now, it feels like we have the upper hand. My whole body tingles. I'm not even worried about the five metalmen that stand between us and the gate.

"Benji?" Soren says, his breaths a wheezing rasp. He's not used to this kind of running. "Now what?"

I cannot fight the grin that finds its way onto my face.

"Stand down," one of the metalmen says, and all at once, the entourage points their broad blades at us, dropping one foot back to assume battle stance. "All lynx imposters and sympathizers are under arrest and will face judgment."

A laugh escapes me. Soren is still looking at me for what to do, so I say, "I think we've faced enough judgment for a lifetime." I readjust my gem staff in my hand. If they don't know the identity of the person behind the mask, they soon will. They cannot see my elation as I turn to Soren. "What do you say we knock some heads one last time on our way out of town, bro?"

Soren flashes me the widest grin I have ever seen.

"I thought you'd never ask."

END OF BOOK ONE

Want to see if Benji and Soren make it out of the capital alive? Find out in Book 2 of **The Fall Gauntlet: RAT**!

www.jamerkel.com

Made in the USA
Las Vegas, NV
02 August 2023

75516059R00038